LAURENT DE BRUNHOFF

BABAR'S COUNTING BOOK

🏠 RANDOM HOUSE

Library of Congress Cataloging-in-Publication Data: Brunhoff, Laurent de. Babar's counting book.
SUMMARY: Babar's three children go for a walk and count what they see. Includes a royal certificate for learning to count to twenty. [1. Elephants—Fiction. 2. Counting] I. Title. PZ7.B82843Babl 1986
[E] 85-19652 ISBN: 0-394-87517-6 (trade); 0-394-97517-0 (lib. bdg.)
Manufactured in the United States of America 1 2 3 4 5 6 7 8 9 0

Early one morning, Babar's children—
Pom, Flora, and Alexander—burst into their parents' room.
"Papa, please come outside!" cried Pom.
"We want to show you that we can count."

"Not now, children," said Babar. "I have work to do. Why don't you run along and count everything you see. I'll join you soon."

The children went for a walk.
"Look over there," said Alexander.
"I see 1 big bird."
Their friend Zephir was hiding in a tree.
He saw the bird too.

1 one

2 *two*

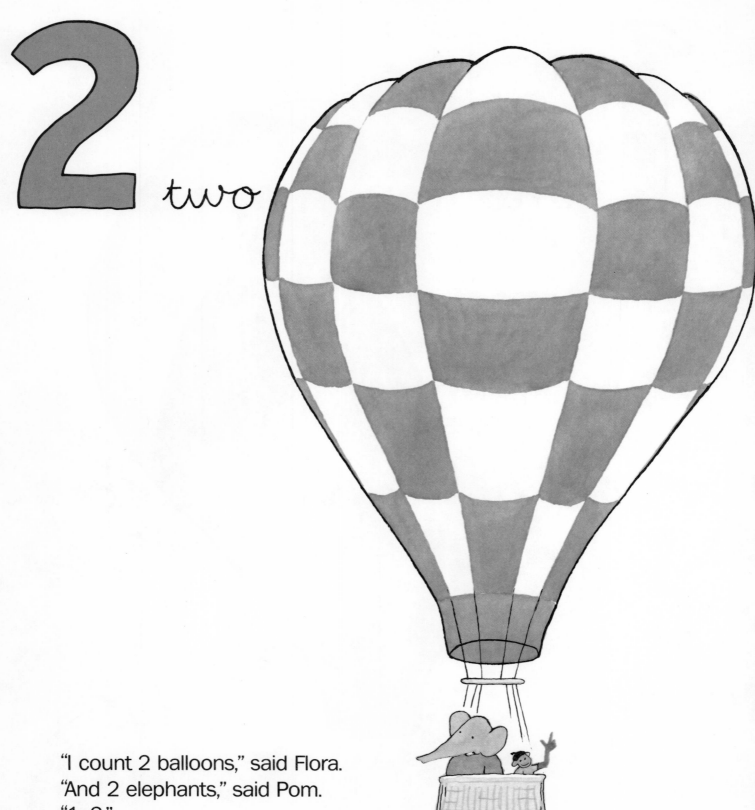

"I count 2 balloons," said Flora.
"And 2 elephants," said Pom.
"1, 2."

3 _three_

Three race cars came speeding by.
Whoosh! Whoosh! Whoosh!
The children had to count fast.
1, 2, 3.

4 four

How many hippos does Pom see?
He sees 4.
1, 2, 3, 4.
How many palm trees can you find?

5 *five*

Flora was sitting in the park.
Five alligators ran past her.
1, 2, 3, 4, 5.
"I wonder where they're going?" she said.

6 six

The alligators were
chasing ostriches.
How many ostriches
were they chasing?
1, 2, 3, 4, 5, 6!

8 eight

Flora heard loud screeches.
"These parrots are so noisy.
There are so many of them!
1, 2, 3, 4, 5, 6, 7, 8."
Can you count them too?

9 nine

Pom was surprised to see so many camels.
He counted them.
1, 2, 3, 4, 5, 6, 7, 8, 9.

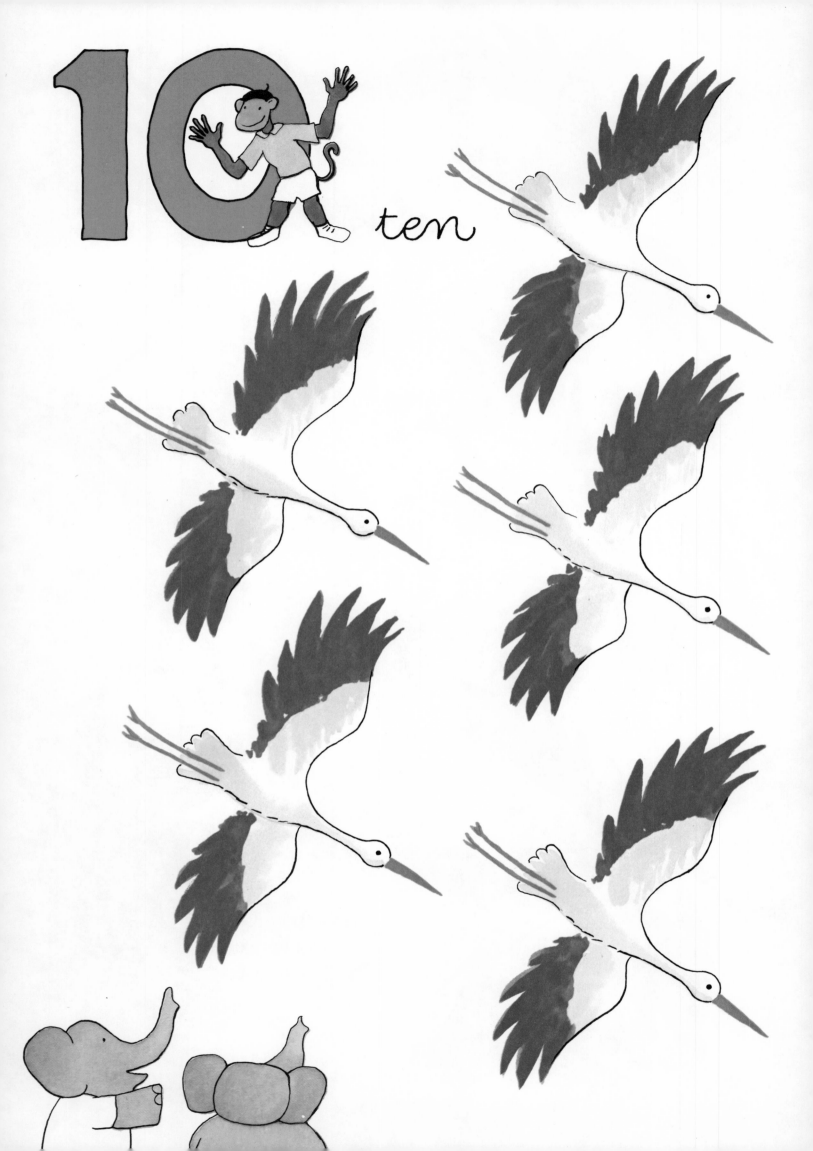

10 ten

Up in the sky,
10 storks flew by.
1, 2, 3, 4, 5, 6, 7, 8, 9, 10.

Babar is very proud of his children.
They can count to 10. Now you can show Babar
how well you can count.

How many alligators are there?
How many balloons? How many butterflies flying?
How many elephants diving and swimming? How many ants?
How many snails creeping by? How many houses are there?
How many camels? How many trees? How many ostriches?
How many dragonflies? How many frogs do you see?
How many cars?

10+1

10+2

10+3

10+4

10+5

10+6

10+7

10+8

10+9

10+10

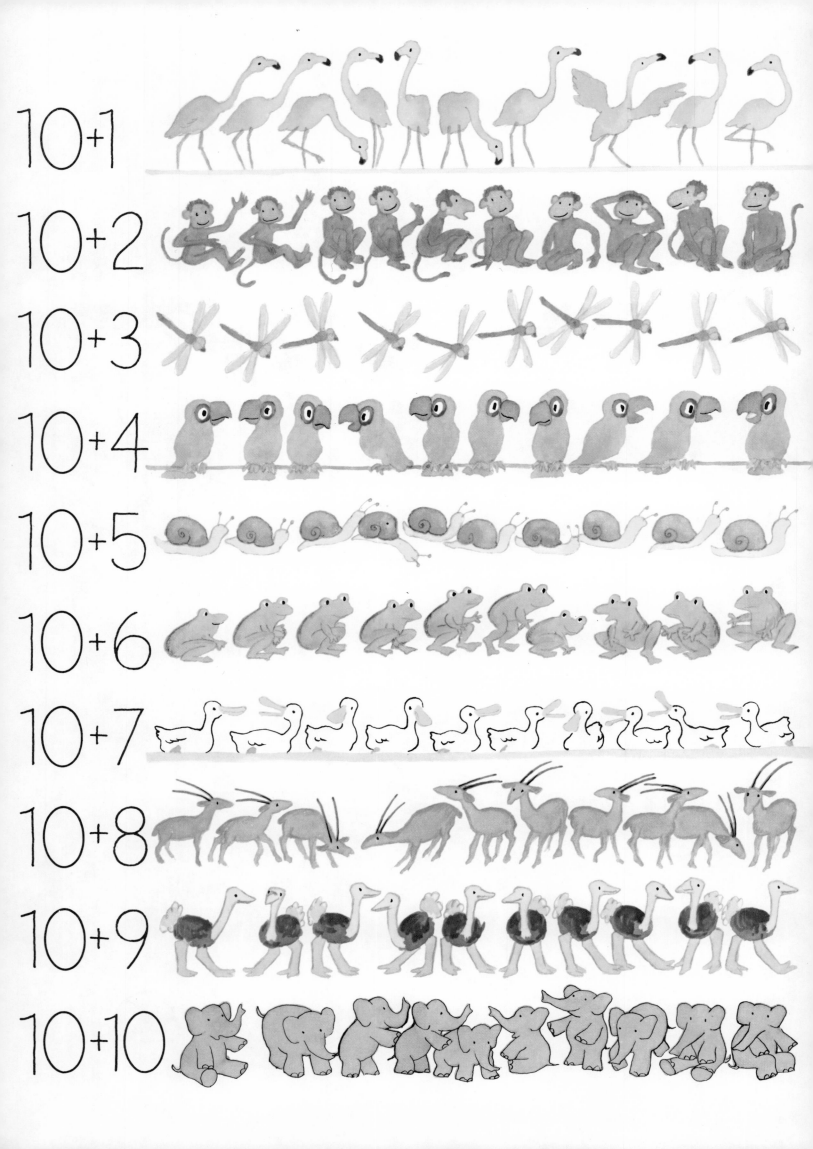

Now Babar shows the children
how to count to 20.
You count too.

eleven

twelve

thirteen

fourteen

fifteen

sixteen

seventeen

eighteen

nineteen

twenty

Babar gives each of the children a royal certificate
because they have learned to count to 20.
There is a royal certificate for you, too.